BENCHED

By Rich Wallace for younger readers:

Sports Camp

Kickers
#1: The Ball Hogs
#2: Fake Out
#3: Benched
#4: Game-Day Jitters

KICKERS

Book 3

BENCHED

by **Rich Wallace**

Illustrated by **Jimmy Holder**

Alfred A. Knopf

New York

Text copyright © 2010 by Rich Wallace
Illustrations copyright © 2010 by Jimmy Holder

All rights reserved. Published in the United States by Alfred A. Knopf, an imprint of Random House Children's Books, a division of Random House, Inc., New York.

Knopf, Borzoi Books, and the colophon are registered trademarks of Random House, Inc.

Visit us on the Web! www.randomhouse.com/kids

Educators and librarians, for a variety of teaching tools, visit us at www.randomhouse.com/teachers

Library of Congress Cataloging-in-Publication Data
Wallace, Rich.
Kickers: benched / Rich Wallace; [illustrated by Jimmy Holder]. — 1st ed.
p. cm.
Summary: Nine-year-old Ben learns some lessons in self-control and sportsmanship when his behavior on the soccer field gets him sent to the bench.
ISBN 978-0-375-85756-0 (trade) — ISBN 978-0-375-95756-7 (lib. bdg.) —
ISBN 978-0-375-89709-2 (e-book)
[1. Soccer—Fiction. 2. Sportsmanship—Fiction.] I. Holder, Jimmy, ill.
II. Title. III. Title: Benched.
PZ7.W15877Kg 2010
[Fic]—dc22
2009034695

The text of this book is set in 15-point Goudy.

Printed in the United States of America
October 2010
10 9 8 7 6 5 4 3 2 1

First Edition

Random House Children's Books supports the First Amendment and celebrates the right to read.

THE BOBCATS

Team Roster

Ben

Mark

Erin

Shayna

Omar

Jordan

Darren

Kim

Coach Patty

CHAPTER ONE
Scraped Up

Ben stared at his quiz paper, trying to remember the capital of Pennsylvania. He knew that it wasn't Pittsburgh. Was it Scranton?

He glanced across the aisle at his best friend Erin's paper, but she hadn't reached that question yet. So he tried to see all the way across the next aisle to Loop's.

"Ben!" his teacher said sharply. "Keep your eyes on your own paper."

Ben looked down. He didn't want to cheat. He just wondered if anyone else was struggling the way he was.

The last state on the list was New York. He wrote *Albany* in the space. He was sure he had eight of the ten capitals right, but he'd left Maine blank. Was it Portland? Or was that the

capital of Oregon? He just couldn't concentrate this morning.

At recess, Ben kept to himself instead of joining his usual game of four square. He hadn't had enough sleep last night. His parents had been arguing about something until nearly midnight.

Mom and Dad had been very quiet at breakfast this morning. Ben could tell that something was wrong.

So he took a seat on a swing and slowly moved back and forth, staring into space and thinking. Usually he'd be running and jumping and burning off energy with the other fourth graders. But right now, he had no energy at all.

A red ball was rolling quickly past. Ben stopped the swing and put his foot on it. When he looked up, Loop was running toward him.

Ben picked up the ball and tossed it to

Loop, who grabbed it with one hand and bounced it. "What are you doing over here?" Loop asked.

Ben shrugged. "Just thinking."

Loop took a step closer and leaned toward Ben. "Eyes on your own paper!" he said, imitating the teacher.

Ben frowned. "Very funny." He and Loop were friends but rivals. They competed hard against each other in sports and games.

"I thought you were the perfect student," Loop said. "What did you do, forget to study?"

"I studied. I was distracted this morning."

"Still thinking about that beating we gave your team a few weeks ago?" Loop said with a laugh.

"Maybe I'm thinking about the beating you'll be getting if you don't shut up." Ben made a fist and held it up.

Loop raised both hands as if to surrender,

but he had a big grin. "Look how scared I am," he said. "I'm shaking."

"Get lost," Ben said. He pumped his legs hard to get the swing moving again.

Loop went back to the four-square game. Ben kept swinging. The October sun was warm on his bare arms.

It was true that Loop's team had shut out Ben's team in a Kickers League soccer game. Ben was still sore about it, but that wasn't the trouble today. Besides, Ben's team had won its most recent game and was in the chase for a spot in the play-offs. It looked as if the Bobcats would get in if they won two of their last three games.

"Ben!"

Ben looked up. Loop was waving him over to the four-square game. "We need you," he called.

Ben could see his classmate Nigel sitting on

the ground with his head back, pressing on his nose. There was blood seeping through his fingers.

"What happened?" Ben asked as he walked over.

"Nigel took a whack in the nose," Loop said. "We need another player."

A teacher came over and helped Nigel to his feet, then led him toward the school. There were drops of blood on the front of Nigel's shirt.

"Did he get hit with the ball?" Ben asked.

Loop shook his head. "The ball was on the line and he and Mark both dived for it."

Ben looked at Mark. Mark frowned and rubbed the top of his head.

"Okay, so what square am I in?" Ben asked.

"First, of course," Loop said.

Ben didn't feel like playing, but they needed at least four for a game, so he stepped in. Then he noticed Erin walking over, so now there would be five players.

When Ben looked back, the ball was already coming toward him. He lunged for it, but it bounced in his square and went out-of-bounds.

"I wasn't ready for that," Ben said.

"Too bad," Loop said. "You were at the square."

"I was here for about half a second!"

"Doesn't matter. If you're at the square, you're ready."

Ben stood still with his mouth hanging open. Then he gave Loop a hard look and stepped to the side of the court. Erin replaced Ben in the first square.

That was no fun, Ben thought, folding his arms. *I might as well go back to the swings.*

But with only five players, he'd be back in the game as soon as this round ended. First chance he had, he'd get back at Loop.

Mark muffed an easy shot and stepped off the court with a sheepish smile. Erin moved up one square and Ben came back in.

The ball moved quickly around the court. Ben knocked it into Erin's square, then returned a volley from Jordan. He was biding his time, waiting for the perfect chance to smack that ball hard into Loop's square.

Here it came. Jordan hit the ball softly and it bounced straight up in front of Ben. Ben whipped the side of his hand into the middle of the ball, chopping it on a line drive at Loop. The ball dipped and just barely caught the inside of the square, then bounced across the playground.

"You're out!" Ben said.

Loop was jogging after the ball, but he turned his head and said, "No way."

"*Yes* way."

"No slams allowed," Loop said. "You know the rules."

"That wasn't a slam," Ben said. "A slam has to bounce higher than your shoulder."

"It did."

"No, it didn't!" Ben took several quick steps to come face to face with Loop. "You're out," he said.

"*You're* out."

"Quit being a baby," Ben said, giving Loop a shove.

Loop shoved back harder.

Ben was in no mood for talking. He took a swing at Loop, hitting him in the shoulder. Loop swung back but Ben ducked.

Head down, Ben wrapped his arms around Loop and tackled him to the pavement. Immediately they were circled by dozens of kids, all yelling at once.

Loop rolled on top of Ben, but Ben dug in with his heels and flipped Loop off of him. Two teachers pushed through the crowd. Mr. Kane grabbed Ben by the shoulders and pulled him away, yelling, "Stop it this instant!"

Ben shook free and glared at Loop. Loop glared back.

"That was a clean shot," Ben said.

"What was? The slam or the punch?"

Mr. Kane stepped between them. "Enough!" he said. "Both of you start marching. Right to Mrs. Nolan's office. Now!"

The principal's office. Ben shut his eyes and scowled. Then he looked down and saw that his pants were ripped below the right knee. His arm was scraped from the pavement.

Loop was scratched up, too.

Mr. Kane followed them to the office. Ben and Loop sat across from each other in folding chairs. They had to wait a long time.

Whenever Ben looked up, Loop was staring at him. Loop mouthed the word "jerk" several times and rubbed a fist into his palm when the secretary wasn't looking. Ben wasn't scared, but he was still angry.

When they finally got into the principal's office, she said, "It seems that there's been a lot of tension over four square lately." She looked directly at Ben. "A lot of it has involved you."

Ben nodded.

"Why is that?" she asked.

Ben jutted his thumb at Loop. "He said I slammed the ball when I didn't."

"That's not what I care about," Mrs. Nolan said. "I've had several reports of arguments, and now this fight. I don't expect that from nine-year-olds. A game isn't worth that kind of distress."

Ben looked at the floor and chewed on his lip. Mrs. Nolan told them they'd be staying in for recess for the rest of the week, and there'd be no four square for either of them for another week after that.

"Now both of you go wash up and get back to class," she said. "Can I trust you to get along?"

"Yes, ma'am," Loop said.

"Yes," said Ben.

Loop walked ahead of Ben along the hallway. He stepped into the bathroom and let the door swing back at Ben. Ben caught it with his scraped-up arm and winced.

There were four sinks. Ben stood at the one farthest from Loop and pushed the soap dispenser, then carefully lathered his arm. He looked into the mirror to see what Loop was up to, but Loop was looking down at the sink.

Loop finished washing and shook his hands rapidly. Then he cleared his throat and pulled some paper towels out of the dispenser. As he dried his hands, he leaned toward the mirror to inspect a tiny cut below his eye. "Maybe that wasn't *quite* a slam," he said.

Ben patted his own scrape with a paper towel. "Yeah, well, maybe I should have been ready for that first serve."

"Then again," Loop said, "it probably *was* a slam. Otherwise I would have returned it." He turned to Ben and grinned. Then he threw the wad of wet paper towels at him.

Ben caught the wad and threw it back. It thumped against a metal trash can and fell to the floor.

"Now *that* was a slam," Loop said.

Ben laughed. "What are we supposed to do all week with no recess? I'll go nuts just sitting in the classroom."

"Me too," Loop said. "Three days of that." He shook his head. "That's what I call distress."

CHAPTER TWO
Too Much Thinking

His mom's car was in the driveway when Ben came home from school. She worked part-time at a bank. Ben arrived at the house before she did a couple of days a week, and he hadn't expected her to be home today.

She was waiting in the kitchen as Ben walked in.

"Hi, Mom!" he said, trying to sound as

upbeat as he could. He walked past her and set his knapsack on the table.

"Come over here," Mom said. She examined the scrape on Ben's arm. Then she put her finger under Ben's chin and tipped his head up. "I had a call from Mrs. Nolan this afternoon."

Ben swallowed hard. He looked back down. "Oh," he said.

"What's the problem, mister? You know better than that."

Ben shrugged. "It was nothing."

"Principals don't call parents about nothing," Mom said. "And boys don't get their clothing and skin cut up from nothing. . . . I thought Loop was your friend."

"He is."

"So why were you two fighting?"

Ben didn't have an answer for that. He knew he'd been feeling rotten all morning.

Surprisingly, he'd felt much better after the fight.

"No answer?" Mom asked.

"Nope."

"Then you'd better spend the rest of the afternoon in your room," she said. "You think about why you were fighting. And think about why you shouldn't."

"I already spent the whole day thinking about it," Ben said.

"Well, go think some more."

Ben lay on his bed with a rubber ball, tossing it toward the ceiling with one hand and catching it with the other. He tried to get the ball as close to the ceiling as he could without actually hitting it.

Tired of that, he opened his dresser and took out the standings for the town soccer league.

NORTHERN DIVISION	Win	Loss	Tie
Rabbits	5	2	0
Sharks	4	3	0
Bobcats	3	3	1
Tigers	2	4	1

SOUTHERN DIVISION	Win	Loss	Tie
Panthers	3	2	2
Eagles	3	2	2
Falcons	3	3	1
Wolves	1	5	1

Ben's team—the Bobcats—would be playing the Tigers on Saturday. The Tigers had won the first time they'd met, back in the opening game of the season. Ben's team had improved a lot since then, but they needed to keep winning. Only the first two teams in each division would qualify for the league play-offs.

Ben glanced out his window. The sun was still shining. He wished he was outside shooting baskets or kicking his soccer ball around the yard.

He heard a knock on his door.

"What?" Ben said sharply.

"It's me." It was Ben's older brother, Larry, who was thirteen.

"Oh."

Larry opened the door. "Heard you had a fight, knucklehead," he said. "Let's see that arm."

Ben held it up. Larry whistled. "That's a nasty scab," he said. "I guess I'm the only one in this house who *hasn't* been fighting lately."

Larry laughed, but Ben didn't think that was very funny. "What was that all about last night?" he asked softly.

Larry shook his head. "I don't know. Mom and Dad were talking about the bills while I was watching TV. It wasn't until after I went to bed that it got heated."

"They *never* fight," Ben said.

"Everybody does. You just don't notice it much because adults fight quietly." Larry smiled. "Unlike you."

Ben scowled. "That was nothing. Me and Loop get mad at each other all the time. It doesn't mean a thing."

"I know. But take some advice: If you're going to get in a fistfight, do it on the grass."

Ben twisted his arm so he could look at his

scrape again. Most of it had started to scab up, but there were still a few scratches that were raw. "There isn't any grass on the playground," he said.

"You could have walked ten feet to the field."

"Sometimes you can't delay it."

"Why not?" Larry asked.

"A teacher would have seen what was happening and broken it up. Loop shoved me. What else was I supposed to do?"

Larry shrugged. "Whatever you say." He sat on the edge of Ben's bed and picked up the ball. He threw it to Ben, who tossed it toward the ceiling again.

"I wouldn't worry too much about last night," Larry said. "Mom and Dad were just working something out, I guess. I heard them say something about credit cards."

"They sure were loud about it."

Larry stood up. "Yeah," he said. He put his

hand on the doorknob but didn't turn it. "I've never heard them yell that much. But like I said, I wouldn't worry about it any more than I would about your elbow. Things like that usually heal pretty fast. Then you forget about it and start over."

CHAPTER THREE
Kicked Out

Ben stared into his cereal bowl on Saturday morning. The flakes were soggy, so he just stirred them around in the milk.

"You'd better eat," Mom said. "You'll have no energy for the game if you don't."

"Can I have something else?" Ben asked quietly. His parents had been arguing again and he had no appetite.

"You could have a banana."

Ben had tried not to listen last night. The argument had something to do with money again. They hadn't been yelling this time, but he could tell from their tone that they didn't agree at all.

"Your father will drive you to the game," Mom said.

"Aren't you coming?"

"I'd like to, but I have to work at the bank this morning," Mom said, patting Ben on the shoulder.

"You never work on Saturdays."

Mom frowned. "I'll be working one Satur-day each month, starting today."

Dad was quiet in the car on the way to the field. He chewed on his lip and looked straight ahead. Ben tried to think about soccer. This was a huge game for the Bobcats.

Ben was late. Both teams were already on the field, with the Tigers in their orange shirts warming up near one goal and the Bobcats at the other, in blue. Ben slammed the car door and sprinted to join his teammates.

Just as he reached them, the referee blew his whistle. "Line up," he called.

"Where've you been?" Coach Patty asked Ben. "I've already set the lineup."

Ben winced. He'd be on the sideline for the start of the game. Usually he'd be at the field at least an hour before a game, but today he'd been moving too slowly. The tension at home was a big distraction.

He knew that he needed to run. Getting into a game or just working hard on his own always seemed to make him feel better.

But Ben stood next to Shayna on the sideline and watched. Shayna was Coach Patty's daughter, but she didn't play any more than anyone else. Ben was glad that the coach treated everyone equally.

He felt a tap on his shoulder and found Loop there beaming. Loop patted himself on the chest. "Guess who's in first place," he said.

"You guys?"

"Yep. Four straight wins. Not bad, huh?"

Ben shrugged. Loop's team, the Falcons, had been in last place a few weeks before, but they were the hottest team in the league.

"We've been moving up, too," Ben said. "If we win this one, we'll be in second in our division."

"I don't think so," Loop said. "The Sharks tied the Rabbits. Nobody thought that would happen."

Ben was surprised, too. The Rabbits were in first place in the Bobcats' division, and Ben had assumed they'd rout the Sharks this morning. The Bobcats were third, behind the Sharks.

"I guess anything can happen," Ben said.

He gulped. The Bobcats would be playing the Rabbits next week. Then they'd finish the season against the Sharks. Two very tough games ahead. That made winning today's game even more important.

Midway through the first half, Coach sent Ben in at forward, replacing Erin. The action had been intense, but neither team had been able to set up a good shot.

These guys are tired, Ben thought. *I'm fresh.* He was sure he could take advantage of that.

But he stumbled the first time he touched the ball, and a few minutes later he passed the ball directly to one of the Tigers. Everyone else was warmed up and into the swing of the game. Ben was playing terribly.

He sprinted toward the player he'd mistakenly passed to, desperate to get the ball back. The kid was circling toward the opposite sideline, moving quickly.

Ben darted over and the Tiger tipped his shoulder, shielding the ball with his body. Ben slid hard, extending his foot between the kid's legs and knocking the ball loose. The kid tripped over Ben's leg and went down. Ben climbed to his feet and ran after the ball.

The whistle blew and the referee pointed at Ben. "That's an illegal tackle," he said. "Tigers' ball. Direct kick."

Ben frowned and jogged back on defense. The field was dry today, and a cool breeze was blowing toward the Bobcats' goal.

The kick went deep into the Bobcats' end of the field, and players scrambled for the ball. A hard shot went directly at Jordan, who was playing goalie. He caught it and punted the ball away.

The teams battled back and forth for the rest of the half, but neither team scored.

"Let's settle down," Coach said as the

players huddled around her. "We seem to have forgotten a lot of what we've learned. Pass the ball, then move to an open space. Stop swarming around the ball so much. And talk to each other out there. If you're open, let your teammates know it."

Ben sat on the bench. Loop walked over and sat next to him. "You guys looked sloppy out there," he said.

Ben stared at the field. He certainly didn't want any advice from Loop. "We'll be fine," he said.

Loop jutted his chin toward the Tigers. "We beat them five–nothing a week ago, and we went easy on them in the second half. They're pretty weak."

Ben checked his shin guards, then stood up and started walking away.

"Then again," Loop said, "they seem to be as good as your team." He laughed.

Ben didn't look back.

Coach put Ben and Erin on defense for the start of the second half, with Mark, Kim, and Jordan up front and Shayna in goal. Ben knew that his first responsibility as a defender was to keep the ball away from the Bobcats' goal, but he planned to be part of the offense, too. He was a fast runner; he could cover the whole field.

Even though the Tigers had possession on their end of the field, Ben ran down to try to steal the ball. An opponent made a nice fake and passed the ball ahead. Two quick passes and a long run moved the Tigers toward the Bobcats' goal.

Ben hustled down the field, but he was lucky that Erin knocked the ball out-of-bounds. He was able to get in position before the throw-in.

Shayna made a save and kicked the ball to Ben. He fielded it on the run and sprinted along the sideline. Two defenders closed in on him and he tried to race past them, but he lost the ball and it bounced to another Tiger.

"Get in control, Ben!" Erin called. "You're playing like a madman."

Ben scowled at Erin and darted toward the ball. He needed to take control all right. Control of the game. It was time for somebody on this team to make something happen.

Ben raised his elbow and pushed an opponent out of the way, then blocked the path of the player with the ball. *I'm taking it*, he thought, smashing into the player with his shoulder and kicking the ball away. *See you later*.

But before Ben could take a single step with the ball, he heard the whistle blast again. The referee was waving a red card at him. "You're out," he said.

"Out?"

The referee pointed toward the sideline. "Out of the game."

Ben put his hands on his hips and looked at his coach. She pointed to the bench. Ben shook his head and walked off the field.

He headed straight for the bench and picked up his water bottle, taking a long drink. The game had restarted, and Jordan had intercepted a pass and was dribbling up the field.

Ben walked over to the coach. "When can I go back in?" he asked.

Coach gave him a slight smile. "Not today."

"Why not?"

"A red card means you're kicked out of the game, Ben. We have to play without you."

Ben's jaw dropped and he looked at the field with his mouth open.

Coach put her hand on Ben's shoulder. "It's great to play hard. But you can't hurt other players. You made two dangerous moves today."

Ben kicked gently at the turf. "I didn't mean to."

"The referee thought you did. That's why he flashed the red card."

Instead of hurting the Bobcats, though, the red card seemed to pump them up. Jordan and Kim made some sharp passes as they moved the ball up the field, and Mark dribbled past two defenders before feeding it back to Jordan in front of the goal. Jordan feinted left, then drove the ball deep into the net. The Bobcats had the lead!

Ben let out his breath. He hadn't even realized he was holding it. He felt horrible that he'd been kicked out of the game, but if his team could win anyway, then maybe they wouldn't be too angry at him.

The Bobcats were playing much better now—passing the ball and playing patient defense. A one-goal lead could disappear in a second, but the Tigers were definitely being outplayed. Jordan had emerged as a very good player over the past few weeks, and every one of the Bobcats had improved. They weren't able to score again, but they did manage to hold on to the lead.

When it ended, Ben stood to the side as his teammates came running off the field. He'd let them down. They were jumping and laughing, having won their third game in a row.

"Play-offs, here we come," said Jordan.

"Watch out, Rabbits," said Erin.

Ben took a seat on the bench and stayed there until all of the players had left except him and Erin.

Then he remembered that his father had driven him to the game. Where was he?

Ben looked around and saw his dad talking to Coach Patty in the parking lot.

"Think they're talking about you?" Erin asked.

"Who else?" Ben replied. He slowly walked over to his father.

"Tough game, huh?" Dad asked.

"It was tough watching instead of playing. I hated that. But at least we won."

"It's worse than you think, Ben," Dad said. "A red card means you have to sit out the next game, too."

"A whole game?"

"A whole game. I wasn't sure if they'd enforce that in this league, but your coach said they do. Red cards are a *big* penalty."

At home, Ben went to his room and took out the standings sheet. He knew the results of all four games from today, so he updated the standings with a pencil. A win over the

Rabbits next week would be a huge step toward the play-offs, but that didn't seem likely since Ben wouldn't be allowed to play.

On the other hand, he hadn't contributed at all today and the Bobcats had won anyway.

Maybe they didn't need him so badly after all.

KICKERS

NORTHERN DIVISION

	Win	Loss	Tie
Rabbits	5	2	1
Sharks	4	3	1
Bobcats	4	3	1
Tigers	2	5	1

SOUTHERN DIVISION

	Win	Loss	Tie
Falcons	4	3	1
Panthers	3	3	2
Eagles	3	3	2
Wolves	2	5	1

Today's scores:

Sharks 2, Rabbits 2

Falcons 4, Panthers 1

Bobcats 1, Tigers 0

Wolves 3, Eagles 2

Next week:

Sharks vs. Tigers

Rabbits vs. Bobcats

Falcons vs. Wolves

Panthers vs. Eagles

CHAPTER FOUR
No Rewards

Ben stayed in his room for the entire afternoon. He was mad about getting kicked out of the game, and he was hungry. He'd had hardly any breakfast and only a small bit of lunch. But it was already four o'clock, so he decided to just wait until dinner. They'd be making their monthly trip to the Chinese restaurant in town tonight.

Ben looked at the list of soccer tips that was

taped to his wall. He'd been writing them down after games and practices. He'd underlined the one that Coach Patty said was the most important: *Always have fun!*

Today hadn't been any fun at all. Ben stretched out on his bed and shut his eyes. He fell asleep.

He dreamed that he was on the soccer field, playing in the championship game. The Bobcats had continued their winning streak, beating the Rabbits and the Sharks and winning their first play-off game. Now they were facing the Falcons for the league title.

The game was tied and Ben had the ball. He was racing toward the goal, and Loop was trying to stop him. The Falcons were throwing red rubber balls at Ben, and Ben was jumping in and out of four-square blocks as he dribbled the soccer ball.

He dribbled through the principal's office

and past a referee who was holding a giant red card. Then he broke into the clear and shot the ball, scoring the winning goal.

He woke up starving. He looked at the clock. It was nearly six.

So he put on his sneakers and headed downstairs.

"Are we leaving soon?" he asked his mom.

"For what?"

"For the Ming Castle."

"Sorry," Mom said. "We decided to eat at home tonight."

"But I wanted sweet-and-sour chicken," Ben said. "I thought that was tonight."

"Usually it would be, but . . . we're making hamburgers instead."

"Oh. How soon? I'm starving."

"We'll eat in about a half hour."

So Ben sat on the couch and watched a

college football game on TV while his stomach growled.

Larry came in and sat next to him. He looked as if he was holding back a smile. "Heard you got booted out of the soccer game," he said.

Ben folded his arms and stared at the TV. "It was a bad call."

"Dad said it looked like you were trying to wipe the guy out."

"I was just going for the ball." Ben sank lower into the couch. The TV screen was focused on a quarterback who'd just fumbled the ball away. He had his helmet off and was looking around as if he was trying to find someone else to blame.

"You're having quite a week," Larry said, and this time he did smile. "Kicked out of recess. Kicked out of soccer. What's next?"

Ben glared at his brother. "It isn't funny."

Larry smacked Ben on the knee. "Hang in there, knucklehead. Things aren't so bad. I went through stuff like that when I was your age, too."

"Why aren't we going out for dinner?" Ben grumbled. "I deserve some wonton soup."

Larry shrugged. "I don't know."

"I guess they're still mad at each other."

Larry raised his eyebrows. They could hear both parents in the kitchen, talking and laughing. "Doesn't sound like it."

"Then why are we stuck here eating hamburgers again?" Ben asked, raising his voice. "We had them on Thursday."

"Maybe because it's cheaper to eat at home."

"I wanted an egg roll."

"You'll survive."

Ben didn't say a word when he got to the

dinner table. Dad had made hand-cut french fries and a big salad, and Mom had broiled a platter of hamburgers. "This'll be nice," she said. "Eating at home can be just as much fun as going to a restaurant."

Ben frowned. He took a hamburger and a big heap of fries. The food was fine, but he liked going out sometimes. This had been a terrible week; he thought he deserved a reward to make up for it.

"Halloween is next Saturday," Mom said. "Have you thought about a costume, Ben?"

He hadn't thought about it at all. Next Saturday was also the day of the game against the Rabbits. The game he'd be sitting out.

"Maybe you can go as a giant red card," Larry said. He and Dad cracked up.

Ben took a bite of the hamburger and looked down at his plate.

"I don't get it," Mom said.

"It's a soccer penalty," Larry said. "Like he got today."

"Oh. . . . Quite a week you've had, Ben."

Ben jutted his chin toward Larry. "That's exactly what *he* said. Why does everybody have to rub my face in it?"

No one said anything more about it, but Ben could see his parents and Larry swapping amused looks. The past few days had been dismal, and the week ahead didn't look any better. No four square allowed, and no chance to play soccer on Saturday.

And what was going on with his parents? Too many arguments this week, and now they were skipping their usual family night at the restaurant.

Things weren't looking good.

So why was everybody laughing but him?

CHAPTER FIVE
Big Talk

Ben wasn't sure if he was allowed at practice, but he went anyway.

"Yes, you can practice with us," Coach Patty said. "The penalty is only for the game."

For once, he didn't feel like practicing, though. After getting kicked out of that game, he didn't even feel like part of the team.

Erin smacked him on the shoulder and said, "Welcome back." She always knew how to make him feel better. Ever since way back in first grade, she could usually make him smile.

But then he remembered that he'd have to sit out an entire game before he could play again for real. "It'll be a drag to sit on the bench and watch you guys on Saturday," he said.

Jordan said, "Keep your head up, Ben. It's only one game."

And Kim added, "The time will fly by like nothing."

But then Ben lined up for a one-on-one drill against Mark. Ben had the ball, and he was supposed to keep it shielded from Mark while dribbling through a set of cones. Mark kept his voice low, but he was hounding Ben the whole time.

"Come on, Mr. Red Card," Mark said. "Watch out for that cone."

Ben had had a number of run-ins with

Mark. Their rivalry had hurt the team early in the season, but lately they'd been playing well together. Now Mark was back to his old ways.

"Watch that elbow," Mark said as they approached the last cone. "Red card . . . red card . . . red card."

Ben circled around the last cone and gave Mark a shove with his hand. "Shut up!" he said.

Mark just laughed and ran back to the start for his next turn.

I can't let him get to me, Ben thought. He knew it was important to stay calm in a game, and that opponents would often try to taunt you. Losing his cool had resulted in that red card.

When the team began scrimmaging, Ben felt more like his old self. He was sweating as they ran the length of the field, and he could feel his heart beating harder. He stole the ball from Jordan, then made a nice pass to Erin and raced toward the goal.

This was more like it.

Here came Erin's pass. It was soft and high, floating toward Ben as he stepped toward the goal. It was at a perfect height for him to head it into the net, and Ben squared his shoulders and jutted his forehead toward it as he jumped.

But Mark was there, too, and he managed to jump higher. Mark was the one who headed the ball, and he sent it down the field, away

from the goal. Ben and Mark collided, and they both fell to the grass.

"Illegal!" Ben said.

"No way!"

"You can't knock me down like that!" Ben yelled.

"I didn't," Mark said. "You ran into me."

Ben scrambled to his feet and chased the ball.

"Mr. Red Card," Mark said again. "You never learn, do you?"

He's still a jerk, Ben thought. *If anybody deserves a red card, it's him.*

The ball flew back and forth, but neither side was controlling it for long. Finally, Ben took a long pass from Erin and headed up the sideline. He dribbled quickly, but he could see Mark coming toward him. Ben ran harder, but Mark was faster, especially since Ben had to keep control of the ball.

Ben was nearly all the way up the field, but he was close to the sideline. None of his teammates were open. Mark was blocking his path to the goal and coming closer, trying to force him out-of-bounds.

"Red card," Mark said softly. "Red card."

Ben stopped short and kicked the ball as hard as he could. He didn't care where it went. "Shut up!" he yelled again. He lunged at Mark, swinging his fist but only hitting the air.

Coach was blowing her whistle, but Ben didn't stop. He dived at Mark this time and wrapped both arms around his waist. Mark spun and they fell to the ground.

Mark broke loose and took a few quick steps away. Jordan and Omar had Ben by the shoulders and were holding him back.

"What's the problem, Ben?" Coach said sharply.

"He won't stop saying 'red card.' "

Coach turned to Mark. "That's very poor sportsmanship," she said. "Ben is your team-mate."

But then she turned to Ben. "If you threw a punch like that in a game, it would cost you more than a red card," she said. "You'd be out of the league for good."

Ben let out his breath. He shook his shoulders free from Jordan and Omar and put his hands on his hips. "He wouldn't shut up."

"Athletes have to stay focused," Coach said. "They can't let *words* throw them off their game. Did Mark trip you?"

Ben looked at the ground. "No."

"Did he elbow you?"

Ben shook his head.

"I didn't think so. All he did was talk, right?"

Ben bit down on his lip and nodded. "Yeah. He's a big talker. And a big jerk."

Coach looked around at the team. "You have to block that stuff out and just play soccer," she said. "The other team, the spectators, sometimes even the other coach, might say something to try to upset you. Don't let it get to you. Stay focused on the game."

Ben looked at Mark, who had a mean smile. He *did* get to Ben, and he knew it.

"Mark, take a seat on the bench," Coach said. "You need to think about being a better teammate. Ben, you should go home. You need to cool off. A lot."

So now he'd been kicked out of practice, too. Ben walked to the sideline and stared at the field as the players began scrimmaging again. It was just three against three. Mark was on the bench with his feet stretched out.

Ben's sweatshirt was on the ground by the bench. Right near Mark.

Ben waited for a minute, then walked over
to get it. This time, fighting hadn't made him
feel better at all. He felt miserable.

Mark kept looking at the field, but he spoke
to Ben. "I was just joking around," he said.

"No, you weren't," Ben replied. "You were
trying to get me mad."

Mark shrugged. "Yeah. I guess that's fun."

Ben shook his head. "Grow up."

"Look who's talking. I'm not the one who keeps getting kicked out."

Ben laughed slightly. "No? Then why are you sitting on the bench?"

"This is temporary," Mark said. "I'll be back on the field in two minutes. But we'll be in trouble on Saturday because of you."

"Because I won't be playing?"

Mark nodded. "Just when we're getting good enough to beat the Rabbits, we have to play without . . . you."

Ben let out his breath and pulled his sweat-shirt on. Out on the field, Jordan was making a breakaway toward the goal. He shifted right, then left, and skillfully shot the ball into the net.

Mark clapped and called, "Nice move!"

With the break in the action, Coach looked over toward the bench. Ben started to walk away. She'd told him to leave, and he didn't want to get in deeper trouble.

"See you at recess," Mark said.

"Yeah," Ben said glumly. "Good luck on Saturday."

"We'll need it."

"I'll be there. On the stupid bench."

Ben didn't turn around until he'd left the park. Mark was back in the scrimmage.

He could blame Mark for today's trouble. He could blame Loop for that fight they'd had at recess last week. And he could blame his parents for the way he'd been feeling, since he was upset about the arguments they'd had.

But he knew who was mostly to blame. He was. And that didn't make him feel any better.

CHAPTER SIX
On the Run

"You're home early," Mom said as Ben entered the kitchen. "Short practice today?"

Ben shrugged. "Yeah, I guess." He opened the refrigerator and looked for something to snack on. He moved a carton of milk and found two leftover chicken legs. "Can I have one of these?"

"Okay, but take it outside. Then wash your

hands so you don't get grease on anything when you come in."

"Who cares about a little grease?"

"*I* do," Mom said. "I've been working extra hours at the bank recently, in case you haven't noticed. So keeping this house clean is a priority for all of us."

Ben went outside and sat on the back steps. *She sure is grouchy lately*, he thought. He bit into the chicken and chewed it slowly, enjoying the salty flavor.

Larry came into the yard. "Hey, squirt," he said. "I thought you had practice today?"

"I did."

"Not us. We've got a race tomorrow, so Coach said we should just jog a little on our own. You want to come?"

Ben thought about that for a second. He was keyed up because his practice had been cut short. "Okay," he said. "How far?"

"Just a mile or two. Nice and easy."

Larry was on the junior high school cross-country team, and he was one of the team's fastest runners.

"I'm all set," Ben said. "I just came from soccer."

"How'd it go?"

Ben grimaced. "Not good."

Larry laughed gently. "I'll be out in five minutes."

They ran slowly down the block and headed to the park where Ben's soccer games were played. There were kids tossing a football around on the field, and other people walking dogs or jogging.

"Just a few easy laps," Larry said. It was the first thing either of them had said since leaving the house.

"So," Larry asked, "what happened at practice?"

Ben stared straight ahead. Suddenly he felt like running a lot faster, but he kept pace with Larry. "Another fight."

"Wow. We'd better get you some boxing gloves."

"This kid just wouldn't shut up about my red card."

"One of your teammates?"

"Yeah."

Larry let out a whistle. "That's bad. Teammates have to support each other, especially when things aren't going well."

"He doesn't know that."

"Do you?"

Ben frowned. "Yeah. . . . But maybe I don't always do it."

They continued on a wide circle around the

field, crossing a bike path and avoiding a muddy area. "Who swung first?" Larry asked.

"I did. But he swung back at me."

"Oh. Is that why you were home early?"

"Yeah. Coach made me leave."

"What about the other kid? Was it that guy Mark?"

"Yeah. She made him sit out for a while, but

he didn't have to leave. We talked on the sideline a little after we calmed down. It was okay."

They left the park and ran on the street for a few minutes until they reached the junior high school. The boys' soccer team was playing, so Ben and Larry stopped by the fence to watch. The team's mascot was dressed in a bear costume and a large green soccer jersey that said LINCOLN. He was dancing and waving his arms, leading the small crowd in a cheer.

"That bear is a riot," Ben said.

The opposing team scored a goal a few seconds later, and the mascot dropped to the ground with his head in his paws. But then he jumped up and waved to the crowd again, getting them to their feet.

"He's got a lot of spirit," Ben said as they jogged toward home.

"*She*," Larry said. "I know her. She's on the

tennis team, but she helps cheer for the football and soccer teams, too."

Ben turned and looked back at the bear. He stumbled as he ran backward, and Larry caught him by the arm.

"I've got a good idea," Larry said. "Saturday is Halloween, right?"

"Yeah."

Ben could see that Larry was fighting back a smile.

"Well," Larry said, "you haven't been a very good teammate lately, but I know how you can make up for it on Saturday."

"You do?"

"Do you have a Halloween costume yet?"

"No," Ben said. "I hadn't thought about it."

"I'll help you make one after dinner tonight," Larry said. "But only if you'll promise to wear it to your soccer game."

Ben thought about it for a moment. He could usually rely on Larry. "Okay," Ben said. "Sounds like a plan."

They reached their house and Larry stopped in the driveway to stretch. Ben sat on the steps and watched him. "How far do you think we ran?" he asked.

"A good two miles," Larry said. "You look like you could run all day."

"I probably could. There's nothing worse than being told *not* to. By a referee or a coach."

"You'll be back in action before you know it."

"I suppose. But being on the sideline for a whole game will be terrible."

"Don't worry," Larry said. "My idea will liven things up."

CHAPTER SEVEN
The Mascot

"Hold still," Mom said as Ben strained his neck to look out the car window. He could see the Rabbits and the Bobcats warming up on the field. The game would be starting in a few minutes, but he was stuck in a parked car while his mother put makeup on his face.

Ben shut his eyes and Mom drew some lines on his cheeks with her lipstick. His nose was already tinted black.

"Do I really have to have red whiskers?" Ben asked, squirming to get away. "I already look stupid enough with these fake ears."

"Yes," Mom said. "Three whiskers on each side. Nice and bright."

Ben reached up to check his headband. It was one of his mother's brown ones, and they'd attached two pointy felt ears to the top to look like a bobcat's. He was also wearing her old leopard-patterned sweatshirt. (The shirt was warm, which helped a lot because the morning was cool.) A short, puffy tail attached to his butt completed the costume.

"Bobcats eat rabbits for breakfast," Ben said as he ran out of the car.

"Don't forget these!" Mom called. She held up a plastic bag filled with slices of orange. Ben had cut them up that morning for his teammates.

"Thanks!" he said, grabbing the bag. He sprinted all the way to the bench.

"What do we have here?" Coach Patty asked. "That's some costume, Ben."

Ben could feel his face get warm from embarrassment. "Just call me Mr. Mascot," he mumbled.

The team gathered around the coach. They were very excited, and seeing Ben in his bobcat costume seemed to give them another lift in spirits.

"This is our most important game yet," Coach said as the players stood in a circle and placed their hands together in the center. "The Tigers beat the Sharks this morning, so our chances are better than ever."

"We're rolling," Jordan said. "Three wins in a row."

"Just get me the ball," Mark said. "We'll show 'em."

"Let's have Ben lead the cheer," Coach said with a laugh, "since he's our biggest fan today."

Ben shook his head and frowned, but he started counting down. "Three . . . two . . . one . . ."

"Bobcats!" they all shouted.

The starters ran onto the field. Erin would be the team's only substitute. None of the Bobcats would get much rest today. Erin punched Ben on the arm and said, "Nice getup."

"This is supposed to get the fans excited," Ben said softly. He looked around. There were kids from other teams sitting in the small set of bleachers, and a few parents of the Bobcats. Ben's mom was standing a few feet away, talking to Erin's parents.

"There aren't very many fans," Erin said. "Don't worry. I'll help you cheer."

Ben shrugged. He had nothing to lose, so he clapped a few times. "Let's go, Bobcats!" he yelled.

"Let's go, Bobcats!" Erin repeated.

Ben walked closer to his mom. "Let's go, Bobcats!" he shouted.

"Go, Bobcats," said the three adults. But then they went back to talking.

Ben turned to the game. The Rabbits had

control of the ball and were moving down the field. Their tactic was to bring all of their players forward except the goalie.

The strategy was working. The Bobcats barely touched the ball in the first few minutes of the game.

Finally, Kim got the ball in the corner and made a nice pass to Mark. He dribbled up the sideline and worked his way past two of the Rabbits. Then he spotted Jordan in the middle of the field, running at full speed toward the Rabbits' goal.

"Here!" Jordan called.

Mark booted the ball on an angle across the field. By the time Jordan ran it down, he was only about twenty feet from the goal. None of the Rabbits had made it back yet, so it was just Jordan against the goalie.

"Breakaway!" Ben shouted.

Jordan made one quick fake and shot the ball toward the goal. The goalie dived, but the shot went cleanly into the net.

Ben leaped and turned to face the bleachers. "J-O-R-D-A-N!" he yelled. "Go, Bobcats!"

"We're looking good," Erin said as the game began again.

"Three wins in a row," Ben said. "Looks like *four*."

But the Rabbits quickly tied the score, and by halftime they'd taken a 2–1 lead. Ben's throat was getting dry from all that yelling.

As the team gathered near the bench, Ben opened the bag of orange slices and handed them out. "Trick or treat," he said. "Come and get it."

Jordan bit into one of the slices and peeled the flesh from the skin with his teeth. "Those guys are *fast*," he said to Ben. "We could use you out there."

"You're doing great," Ben said. "Keep the pressure on them."

"They're the best passers we've played against," said Kim. "Even better than the Falcons."

Ben looked out at the field, which was scuffed up from all the recent games. The grass had turned brown a few weeks before, and the nearby trees had shed a lot of colorful leaves.

The game started again, and Ben went back to his yelling-and-jumping routine. But then he settled down and watched. The Rabbits' best players were patient with the ball, making accurate passes and working together. They never appeared to panic, even if Mark or Kim or Jordan made a run toward the goal with the ball.

Midway through the second half, the Rabbits' steady play paid off in another goal. They had a 3–1 lead. Ben could see the disappointment on his teammates' faces. They started playing with less excitement. The game seemed to be lost.

Ben clapped loudly. "That's not the Bobcat spirit!" he shouted. "Mark! Shayna! Omar! Let's go! There's plenty of time left in this game."

Ben's enthusiasm seemed to make a difference. He could see a spark as Jordan took control of the ball and raced up the field. He sent a crisp pass across the grass to Kim, who turned and fired it back.

Jordan was in the clear as he ran past Ben near the sideline.

"Looking great!" Ben shouted. "Kim and Mark are with you."

A Rabbit defender ran up to Jordan, who stopped short and dodged to his left. As the Rabbit went for the fake, Jordan shifted to his right and dribbled toward the goal.

Mark and Kim moved quickly into the goal area, waiting for a pass or a rebound. Jordan was at a tough angle to make a shot, but he was in perfect position to pass. He kicked the ball to Kim, who had a dead-on shot at the goal.

The Rabbit goalie crouched low, ready to spring at the ball. Kim planted her left foot and swung back her right. And then she did something really special.

Instead of shooting, she nudged the ball over to Mark. Mark trapped it and shot it past the goalie.

"Yes!" Ben cried. "We got it right back! One more and this game is tied."

Ben wiped his forehead and let out his breath. He was puffing and sweating as much as if he'd been playing. He slapped hands with Darren, who was waiting to get back into the game.

"When you get in there, you need to hustle like never before," Ben said.

Darren nodded. He was the quietest Bobcat. Coach sent him onto the field and Jordan came out.

"Just a short breather," Coach said to Jordan. "Catch your breath and we'll get you right back in there."

Jordan walked over to Ben and held up his hand for a high five. "It's intense out there," he said.

"Way to get that goal right back," Ben said. "For a second, I thought we were hanging it up."

"I heard you yelling," Jordan said. "Thanks. That gave us a lift."

Ben shrugged. "Not much else I can do. Not in this game anyway."

Coach called Jordan over a few minutes later. Ben went, too.

"This is it, Jordan," she said. "We've got about three minutes left to tie this game. Go in for Omar at the next whistle."

Ben tapped Jordan on the shoulder. "Run!" he said. "Don't stop running until the game ends."

The Rabbits had control of the ball and were biding their time with it. They didn't need to score. If they could let the clock run out, they'd walk off the field with a victory. The Bobcats had to put the pressure on.

"Attack the ball!" Ben called.

Erin was playing goalie for the Bobcats, but the other five had all moved up the field. The Rabbits were playing an effective game of keep-away, but the Bobcats were guarding them closely.

Finally, Shayna intercepted a pass and kicked the ball back to Darren. Mark and

Jordan both yelled for it, and Darren sent it across to Mark.

Mark was faster than most of the Rabbits, and he raced along the sideline across the field from Ben. Ben ran in the same direction. So did all of the players on the field.

Mark would often lose control of the ball when he tried to dribble long distances. And he was much more likely to shoot than to pass, even if he didn't have a clear path to the goal.

But maybe this was one time when Mark's selfishness would pay off. There wasn't much time left in the game. The Bobcats had to score.

Mark approached the goal and fired the ball from a tough angle. The Rabbit goalie blocked it with both hands, but he couldn't hold on. The ball bounced to the side of the goal.

Jordan reached it first. He pivoted and shot, but the ball bonked off the goalpost and rebounded onto the field. A Rabbit stopped it with his chest and let it drop to the ground. As he tried to sweep it away, Kim ducked in and stole it.

The goalie and two other defenders were between Kim and the goal. She darted to her right, stepped over the ball, and slid it with the outside of her foot toward the front of the goal. Mark was there. He shot it hard, but right into the hands of the goalie.

The goalie kicked it long and hard. All six Rabbits and five Bobcats were near the goal, so no one was at the other end of the field except Erin.

Usually the goalie would stay near the goal, of course, but Erin ran up the field and took control of the ball. There was less than a

minute remaining. She could add some power to the Bobcats' attack.

"You're on offense now!" Ben shouted.

Erin was past midfield before any of the players reached her. She passed the ball to Jordan, who kicked it to Kim, near the corner.

Kim lofted the ball into the air and it fell directly in front of the goal. Shayna shot, then Mark, but the goalie blocked them both. When a Rabbit defender kicked the ball back across midfield, the referee blew the final whistle.

The Rabbits had held on to win, 3–2.

"Best effort so far this season," Coach said as the exhausted Bobcats flopped onto the grass and the bench. "Awesome work."

Jordan was staring at the turf. Mark had his eyes shut with his face toward the sky. Kim was pacing and gazing at the Rabbits' goal. None of the Bobcats looked happy about the effort. They'd lost.

So close, Ben thought. *So close to the best team in the league*.

He slowly removed the headband with the bobcat ears. He stared at it for a few seconds. If they'd been that close with only seven players, how would they have done with eight?

CHAPTER EIGHT
Play-off Pressure

At dinner that night, Mom kept talking about what a great mascot Ben had been. "So enthusiastic," she said. "You guys should have seen him."

"Too bad we missed it," Dad said. "But Larry had a race, and I was too busy catching up on some reports for work."

Ben swirled his spaghetti with his fork. "Are

you too busy to go trick-or-treating with me tonight?" he asked.

Dad laughed. "Not too busy, but maybe too old."

"I'll take you," Larry said. "Maybe we could go for a trick-or-treating *run*."

"Nah. I'd spill all my candy."

"That's okay," Larry said. "I've run enough

for one week . . . We won the race this morning, by the way."

Mom cleared her throat. "Speaking of being busy . . ."

Ben set down his fork.

"I've decided to start working full-time at the bank," Mom said. "That means you'll get home before I do every day after school, Ben. And I'll have to work some Saturday mornings, too."

"How come?" Ben asked. She'd been working three days a week since he'd started school.

"We need the money," she said. "I'm sure you've noticed some tension between me and Dad lately. I think it's part of the reason you've been getting yourself into trouble at school and at soccer."

Ben nodded. "Maybe," he said.

"Money doesn't make anyone happy," Mom said, "but it can make you tense. We need for me to earn more of it. So that's why I'll be working more."

"Sounds okay," Ben said. "Hey, does that mean we can start going to the Ming Castle again?"

Mom smiled. "Are you getting tired of spaghetti and hamburgers?"

"A little."

"We'll go next Saturday night," Dad said. "That'll be a day to celebrate. Larry has the county cross-country championships in the morning, and it'll be the end of Mom's first full-time week at the bank."

"Big day for me, too," Ben said. "I finally get to play soccer again. I've missed a game and a half because of that stupid red card."

"We're all glad that's over," Mom said. "I think you earned your way back onto the field with that cheering display this morning."

"Yeah, that was fun," Ben said. "But not nearly as much fun as playing."

The evening was cool and breezy, so Ben put an extra sweatshirt under his bobcat costume and added a pair of brown mittens. Larry put on an old Wolfman mask, and they headed out to the street.

They trick-or-treated at several houses in the neighborhood, then reached Erin's. She answered the door in a rabbit costume.

"Hey," Ben said. "How come you're dressed like our enemies?"

"I hadn't even thought about that," Erin said. "Besides, that game is done. Our new rivals are the Sharks."

"Yeah," Ben replied. "It's going to be like a championship game. Whoever wins goes to the play-offs. The loser is finished for the season."

Erin joined them for another half hour of trick-or-treating. All Ben wanted to talk about was next week's game.

"We beat the Sharks last time," he said. "And we're a lot better now."

"Every team in the league is better," Erin said. "Remember, the Sharks tied the Rabbits last week."

"But they lost to the Tigers today. The Tigers are in last place."

"It just shows you that any team can win any game," Erin said. "We'll have to play better than ever to beat the Sharks."

Ben was ready to do that. Watching today's game had been hard. Every time the Bobcats had the ball, he wanted to run onto the field and set up for a shot. It had been frustrating to do nothing but cheer.

But he'd also noticed some things that he might not have seen if he'd been in the game. Players still tended to bunch up near the ball instead of getting to an open area for a pass. Both teams moved in a swarm sometimes. And many of the players tried to do too much when they had the ball, forcing their way through a pack and usually losing control of the play. Ben had seen lots of missed chances for passes.

"What if the game ends in a tie?" Erin asked. "We both have the same record. Who gets the play-off spot then?"

Ben shrugged. "I have no idea, but I'm not worried about it. We'll win. A *big* win, and then we'll get ready for the play-offs."

At home, Ben took another look at the league standings. The Rabbits and Falcons were assured of making the play-offs, no matter what happened in their next games.

KICKERS

NORTHERN DIVISION

	Win	Loss	Tie
Rabbits	6	2	1
Sharks	4	4	1
Bobcats	4	4	1
Tigers	3	5	1

SOUTHERN DIVISION

	Win	Loss	Tie
Falcons	5	3	1
Panthers	4	3	2
Eagles	3	4	2
Wolves	2	6	1

Today's scores:

Rabbits 3, Bobcats 2

Tigers 4, Sharks 3

Falcons 5, Wolves 1

Panthers 4, Eagles 2

Next week:

Wolves vs. Panthers

Eagles vs. Falcons

Bobcats vs. Sharks

Tigers vs. Rabbits

Watch out, Sharks, Ben thought as he took off his bobcat costume and got ready for bed. *No more mascot. And no more red cards. Next week will be the best game of my life.*

He picked up a pen and added another tip to the list on his wall. *Getting angry or frustrated won't help you play better.*

CHAPTER NINE
Hamburger and Butterfly

Things went well for Ben over the next few days. He played four square at recess every day. He was rusty at first because he hadn't been allowed to play for more than a week, but by Wednesday he was at the top of his game.

He got an A on a history test. And at soccer practice, he scored two goals during a scrimmage.

But every night in bed, he stared at the

ceiling for a long time, thinking about the upcoming game against the Sharks.

Finally, the day arrived. He was up early, so he walked to the field. He was one of the first players to get there, even though there were two games before the Bobcats would play.

He watched the Panthers beat the Wolves. Every few minutes, he ran the length of the field. Not too fast. He wanted to save his energy, but he seemed to have too much of it.

During the second game, Ben did jumping jacks and sit-ups. The Falcons were routing the Eagles. Ben could hear Loop's voice throughout the game, shouting for the ball. Loop tended to be loud on the field, but he was a strong player. He and his teammate Alex had become the best combination in the league, setting each other up for many goals.

Ben's teammates began arriving, so he stood

near the sideline with Jordan and Kim and Erin. None of them said much. They were all thinking hard about what they had at stake.

"Big one today," Jordan finally said.

"The biggest," Ben replied. He could see players from the Sharks gathering on the other side of the field. Their yellow soccer shirts were easy to spot.

Ben had scored the winning goal the first time the Bobcats played the Sharks. That seemed like a long time ago. With just seconds left in the game, the goalie had blocked Shayna's shot. The ball rebounded onto the field and Ben reached it first. He turned and scored—his first goal ever.

That had been more than a month ago. Now Ben watched as Loop's team ran off the field with another victory, their sixth straight. The rematch was about to begin.

Ben looked around and saw that his parents had arrived. He raised his fist and smiled. Mom shouted, "Go, Bobcats!"

Ben couldn't contain his energy much longer. He bounced up and down as he and Jordan and Kim waited on the front line for the game to begin. *Calm down,* he thought. *Don't be too aggressive.*

Coach had put Erin and Mark on defense, with Darren as goalie. Omar and Shayna waited near the bench.

The first time Ben touched the ball was after a short pass from Erin. He turned and looked for a place to run, but his path was blocked by two of the Sharks. He stepped over the ball and swept it toward the sideline, but a defender with yellow wristbands charged in and knocked it loose with his foot. The other Shark took possession and moved into the Bobcats' end of the field.

Ben stumbled but caught himself before he fell. "He tripped me," he muttered. He took a quick look at the referee, who did not blow his whistle. It was the same referee who had thrown him out of the game against the Tigers.

Ben glanced over at his parents. Dad shook his head and called, "Don't let it bother you."

A few minutes later, Ben got hit again. Jordan dribbled across midfield and sent a smooth pass a few yards in front of Ben. Ben ran to the ball and nudged it forward, picking up speed as he went.

Those same two Sharks moved into his path, one on either side. Ben gave a quick fake and dodged past the first one, but the second stepped closer. Their knees collided, and Ben felt a sharp pain. The ball squirted away.

Where's the foul? Ben thought. He glared at the referee, but again there was no whistle.

Ben stopped and rubbed his knee. These guys were playing rough.

"Are you all right?" Coach called.

Ben nodded and ran toward the ball. *Keep calm*, he thought. *Don't let them get to you.*

The player he'd knocked knees with had the ball. With Mark approaching, the kid had slowed down and was looking for someone to pass to.

Ben could see the play developing as another Shark drifted back and called for the ball.

That's mine! Ben thought as the pass was made. He darted toward the ball and took control before it reached the other Shark. With room to work now, Ben raced up the field.

He cut toward the middle to avoid a defender, then caught sight of Kim coming up to his right. He passed the ball in her direction, but it was too far ahead of her. It rolled out-of-bounds and a Shark ran toward it for a throw-in.

"Nice pass, Red," said the kid with the yellow wristbands.

Ben was startled. "What did you call me?"

"You heard me," the kid said with a smirk. "We know all about your red card."

The Sharks seemed to be doing everything they could to upset Ben. They were elbowing and tripping him and calling him names.

I'm not getting caught up in that nonsense, Ben thought. They could try to bait him, but it wouldn't work.

The Bobcats made a couple of nice runs toward the goal, although Jordan's shot was blocked and Kim's went just wide of the net.

"We're the better team," Ben said to Kim after her miss. "Keep it up."

But the breaks didn't seem to be with the Bobcats today. Despite outplaying the Sharks for most of the half, they didn't manage to score. And when the Sharks put the ball past Darren and into the goal in the final minute of the half, Ben felt his stomach sink.

All that work and we're behind, he thought as he walked off the field at halftime. The rest of the Bobcats looked stunned, too.

Ben took a seat on the bench and felt his knee. He'd played the entire half, so he hadn't had a chance to examine it. There was a red spot on the side and it was sore when he pressed on it. But it hadn't slowed him down.

Jordan joined Ben on the bench. "We can't play much better than that," he said.

"The only thing missing was some goals," Ben replied. "We should have had a couple."

"Just keep working," Jordan said. "Sooner or later the shots will go in."

"They'd better. I'm not ready for this season to be over."

"Neither am I," Jordan said.

Ben rapped his knuckles on the bench. "They kept trying to get on my nerves," he said.

"Me too," Jordan replied. "One guy was calling me Butterfly."

"Why would he call you that?"

Jordan shrugged and smiled. "Who knows? Would *you* like being called that?"

"I don't even get it."

"Neither do I. 'Come on, Butterfly,' he kept saying. 'Don't lose that ball, Butterfly.' "

Ben laughed. "That's ridiculous."

"I know. But it *was* very distracting."

"They called me Red."

Mark had come up behind them. "They called me Hamburger," he said. "I was ready to punch somebody at first. Then I just got fired up about the game."

"We're better than they are," Jordan said. "They can call us whatever they want. But at the end of the game, they'll be calling us winners."

Jordan stood on the bench and waved the rest of the team over. "Listen up," he said quietly. "We've got twenty minutes left in this game. Twenty minutes left in the season if we

don't put that ball into the net a few times. Who's ready?"

"We are," said the Bobcats.

"Who is?"

"We are," they said more loudly.

"Are you sure?"

"Yes!" they yelled.

Jordan stepped down from the bench. "Hands in here," he said. They all reached in, just as they did before every game. "We win or we go home. One . . ."

"Never stop running," Ben said.

"Two . . ."

"Use every ounce of strength," Ben added.

"Three . . . Bobcats!"

CHAPTER TEN
More Trash-Talking

"Here's the lineup for the second half," Coach Patty said. "We need some goals, so let's really hustle.

"Shayna's been our top goalie all season, so she'll play there. Mark, Erin, and Kim will start at forward, and Darren and Omar will rotate in and out with them. You forwards need to work like never before.

"Ben and Jordan will be on defense. That

might sound strange since you're both great scorers, but I'm counting on you to play both ends of the field. Your first role is to stop the Sharks from getting close to our goal, but I also want you to be part of our offense."

The strategy worked well. At least it kept the Sharks from scoring another goal. But as hard as they tried, the Bobcats weren't able to get close to scoring, either. The minutes ticked away. Ben felt as if he'd sprinted several miles.

The Sharks were keeping up their banter as well as their hard play. Ben heard "Red" every time he touched the ball, and also "Hamburger" and "Butterfly" when his teammates had it. Kim was now being called String Bean. Erin was French Fry.

Those are the stupidest insults I've ever heard, Ben thought as he ran toward the ball. But he knew that they were working. Although the Bobcats were playing very hard, they seemed disorganized. It was hard not to listen to those silly names.

The Sharks were killing a lot of time by making safe passes back and forth, not even attacking the goal. But then Mark fell on the grass and a Shark slipped past him with the ball. He made a quick pass to an open team-mate, who fired the ball at the goal.

Shayna had to dive to stop the ball. She batted it with both hands and it rolled to the side. Another Shark ran toward it and booted it hard.

Shayna was still on the ground. Erin had dropped back and was in front of the goal. She couldn't use her hands, but she managed to get a foot on the ball and deflect it away.

Again the Sharks got control. Two quick passes led to another shot, and Shayna made her second great save in a matter of seconds. This time, the ball wobbled out-of-bounds to the side of the goal. The Sharks would be putting the ball into play with a corner kick.

"We're getting bombarded," Jordan said.

"Toughen up!" Ben called.

The corner kick floated in the air for a long time and finally came down in front of the goal. Mark caught it on his chest and let it drop, then booted it as hard as he could.

The kick was off-center, and the ball spun toward the sideline. Jordan scooted over to it and directed it up the field, chasing after it.

Jordan had a wide-open field in front of him and he kept moving. He passed the midfield line and ran deep into the Sharks' territory. Mark and Ben, the two fastest Bobcats, were running up the field, too. They were spread wide but were even with Jordan. Only two defenders and the goalie were in their way.

The defenders were the same two kids who'd given Ben trouble in the first half. They shifted forward a bit, closing the gap on Jordan.

As Jordan neared the goal box, he stopped short and leaned to his right. Then he made a quick move to the left, drawing both defenders toward him.

"Hamburger!" yelled Mark, who was directly in front of the goal.

Jordan passed the ball to Mark. As the defenders ran toward him, Jordan shouted, "Butterfly!"

Mark slid the ball back to Jordan.

Ben sprinted to the front of the goal. Jordan sent a soft, high pass into the air. Ben planted his feet. The goalie and the nearest defender were taller than he was.

I can outjump them, Ben thought. He leaped as the ball came down, meeting it squarely with his forehead. The ball made a line drive into the goal.

Ben had tied the score! He turned to the kid with the yellow wristbands. "Red!" he yelled. Then he ran to Jordan, jumping again and bumping his chest against his teammate's.

"We turned that around," Jordan said. "We threw those insults right back in their faces."

Ben, Mark, and Jordan ran back to the Bobcats' end of the field, slapping each other's palms as they went. "Hamburger!" "Butterfly!" "Red!" they shouted in turn.

The referee brought the ball to the midfield circle so the Sharks could put it back into play. But then he raised his hand and blew his whistle.

The ref waved for all of the players to join him in the circle. He had a thick gray mustache but not much hair on his head.

"What's going on?" Jordan asked.

"That can't be the end of the game," Ben said. "Let's go up and see."

"Just a caution," the referee said when all the players were there. "I'm hearing too much trash-talking in this game. There's a lot on the line, but let's decide the outcome with our soccer skills, not our big mouths."

Ben looked over at the kid with the wristbands. He was looking back at Ben from the other side of the circle. Ben blushed a bit and looked away.

The referee smiled. "There's just under three minutes to go," he said, "and the game's tied." He stepped out of the circle and blew his whistle.

The Sharks put the ball into play. They controlled it for nearly a minute, then lost the ball out-of-bounds.

Mark made a long throw-in, but Kim had the ball stolen before she reached midfield.

The Sharks brought the ball down the field and took a weak shot. Shayna scooped it up and punted it high. Ben drifted under it, keeping his eyes on the ball. As it came down, he tensed his shoulders and puffed out his chest, waiting to trap it.

Just as the ball arrived, Ben felt a shove. He shoved back with his arm and the ball bounced off the ground, continuing up the field.

"Sorry," said the Shark with the wristbands.

"No problem," Ben said as they both chased the ball.

Ben got to it first.

"Trailing!" called Erin, who was coming up behind. Ben knocked the ball backward, then moved away as the defender turned toward Erin.

Get open! Ben told himself.

Erin sent the ball back to Ben, and he took off with it at a sprint. He could see Jordan coming up the middle of the field, but he wanted to lure the last Shark defender away before passing.

Just as expected, the Shark ran toward Ben. After two more steps, Ben passed the ball along the grass, angling it in front of Jordan.

Jordan took the ball without breaking stride. Ben ran toward the goal, too, but he never took his eyes off Jordan. The only Shark between Jordan and the net was the goalie.

"Trailing!" Ben called, but Jordan didn't need help. He made a series of quick fakes that left the goalie reeling. Jordan shot the ball deep into the corner of the net.

Ben dropped to his knees and shut his eyes. He raised both fists, then leaped up and grabbed Jordan in a bear hug. The Bobcats had the lead. If they could hold it for another minute, they'd be in the play-offs.

"Everybody back!" Ben yelled. "Defense!"

The Sharks brought every player up, including the goalie. They were desperate to tie the score. Ben and Jordan chased the ball

wherever it went, and the rest of the Bobcats stuck close to the other opponents.

A pass across the center of the goal box looked dangerous for a second, but Kim ran up and kicked the ball the length of the field. It rolled across the end line. Two of the Sharks sprinted back to get it, but the play killed a lot of time.

When the final whistle blew, Ben shut his eyes again. He wanted to shout, but he couldn't even speak. It had been a while since he'd felt this happy. Erin smacked him on the shoulder, and even Mark said, "Great game, Ben."

Ben nodded. He'd played his best game of the season. He was shouting with joy inside.

He hugged Jordan and Erin, then hacked up some saliva that was stuck in his throat.

"Great game, *Red*," Erin said. "Can you believe it? We did it!"

"We earned it, *French Fry*," Ben replied with

a laugh. "That was our toughest game, but it was the hardest we ever played, too."

"Next week will be even tougher," Erin said. "I've never been in any kind of play-off before."

"Me either. But I already can't wait."

Ben looked around at the tired players from both teams. Everyone had played their hearts out.

He and Erin led the way as the Bobcats walked to midfield to shake hands with the Sharks. When Ben reached the kid with the wristbands, he shook extra hard. The guy was a great competitor.

They tried to upset me with all the trash-talking, Ben thought. *But I kept my mind on the game.*

Because of that, the Bobcats had made it to the play-offs.

BEN'S TOP TIPS FOR SOCCER PLAYERS

• Let the ball do the work. Keep it moving by passing it.

• Talk to your teammates on the field, letting them know when you're open. Call "Trailing!" if you're coming up from behind, for example.

• Pass to a player who has space to work with, not one who is tightly guarded by an opponent.

• Keep control of your emotions. Getting angry or frustrated won't help you play better.

• The most important rule: Always have fun!